Secret of the Starflower
Rainbow of Spectra

Rainbow of Spectra

Published by Jessica Kopecky Design, LLC

Visit the author's website:
www.secretofthestarflower.com

ISBN: 978-1-7369641-1-8 (eBook)
ISBN: 978-1-7369641-0-1 (Paperback)

Library of Congress Control Number: 2021940371

JUVENILE FICTION/Animals/Dragons, Unicorns & Mythical

Version 2021.06.07

To Josie
My inspiration, co-author and cheerleader

And My Mum
*For all the big and small ways you've supported
my hair-brained ideas*

All of us are given special gifts.

That's why we need each other.

~ Stella

Part 1 - LIES

Part 2 - TRUTHS

Look out for **bold** *colors throughout the story to learn new words in the glossary!*

Secret of the Starflower
Rainbow of Spectra

Written and Illustrated by

JESSICA KOPECKY

Jessica Kopecky
DESIGN

Part 1
LIES

Chapter 1:
On Her Own

Sandy was hiding.

She peeked through a coral, checking overhead for chomperfish the way her father taught her when she was a filly. Remembering his lessons had kept her safe since she hugged her parents goodbye.

She kept her rainbow mane out of sight by swimming close to the sand, underneath the branches of coral in her multicolor reef.

The life of a seahorsicorn was supposed to be simple. If they could avoid the hungry jaws of chomperfish and keep their bellies full of plankton, they were free to swim together and be merry. For most of the citizens in Spectra, that was easy.

Sandy tried to blend in like the others—she really did—but her rainbow mane always got in the way. It all started when she failed her first lesson in school, Coral Safety.

When the other fillies and colts closed their eyes and focused on their magic, their horns warmed up, sparkled, and then—the seahorsicorn would vanish! But when Sandy tried, she couldn't do it. Instead, a starflower appeared on the coral next to her.

"Ha," said her yellow schoolmate Cynthia, "Her rainbow mane makes her magic broken! One-color manes are better!" The classmates

joined her for a cruel laugh.

To make matters worse, the teacher warned the class that her rainbow mane was a target for hungry chomperfish.

"Chomperfish are attracted to bright flashy... things..." she said, looking down her snout at Sandy. Then, turning her gaze to the rest of the classroom, she announced, "If you want to stay safe, you'll distance yourself from anything too... noticeable."

None of Sandy's schoolmates wanted to be near her after that.

After school Sandy fell into her mother's arms. "Why is my magic broken?" she asked as she released salty tears into the salty ocean.

"Your magic isn't broken," her mother reassured her. "It's just different."

"But Spectra is covered in starflowers. Who needs more of those? What I really need is to disappear! My stupid hair makes my magic useless!"

Her mother stroked her mane, then said, "Legend says the Great Spirit used to give out different gifts, not just disappearing magic. Maybe your magic isn't broken. It could be a blessing."

Sandy tried to believe she was blessed,

but she felt cursed instead.

As her hair grew brighter and longer, the chomperfish often spotted her. She was forced to swim for her life, starflowers popping up all around her as she desperately tried to make disappearing magic work. Meanwhile, she could hear the others laughing from their invisible hiding places.

Sandy's parents protected her by gathering her meals while she stayed safe in the nest. As they added four little siblings to the family, Sandy could tell by their tired faces that her daily food needs had become a burden.

When they ventured out together for important seahorsicorn festivals and gatherings, her steadily growing mane exposed her family to the chomperfish.

Finally, Sandy insisted on leaving; it was the right thing to do. So she struck out on her own, skittering here and there, doing her best to hide until she could figure out how to build her own nest and feed herself.

Sandy dashed from the coral to a seaweed patch, her unruly mane and satchel of belongings trailing behind her. As she wove through the weeds, she found a couple stray plankton to eat, but her stomach ached for more. She had only found a few plankton since she left the nest the day before.

The best place to find food was out in the open, where gentle currents carried plankton through like a lunch buffet. Seahoricorns plucked them effortlessly from the water and munched to their heart's content. Sandy didn't dare join such a feast, because that meant exposing herself to the chomperfish... and the others.

But today her stomach growled, and

the plankton dinner attracting a gathering of seahorsicorns was too mouthwatering to resist. She spied an opening between two young stallions and meekly wiggled her way through, hoping no one would notice.

Once she tasted the fresh open-water plankton, her hooves grabbed at the current in a wild frenzy as she stuffed her face. While she filled her empty belly, she caught the attention of a young stallion next to her. He reared back in shock.

"Sandy?" He bumped into the seahorsicorn next to him. Several of them looked at her mane and backed away in fear.

She covered her snout with her hooves. "I'm sorry," she said through pursed lips that held back cheekfuls of food. But it was too late. The others had already taken notice.

It wasn't just her old classmates who rejected her. The entire seahorsicoral had seen the way the chomperfish chased her. Elderly seahorsicorns glared at her. A mother gasped and held her foal tightly.

As the crowd parted, Cynthia stood glaring at Sandy with the usual flicker of spitefulness in her eyes. Her girlfriends surrounded her.

"Oh, no!" thought Sandy. It was bad enough that the others were afraid of her, but Cynthia was just plain mean.

"Sandy! You ruin everything! This was a perfectly good meal until you showed up! No one wants to be gobbled up by chomperfish, freak! I hope you're happy eating by yourself!"

Cynthia and her friends turned their backs to Sandy, tossing their beautiful one-color manes over their shoulders. All but Sammi, a soft-spoken pink mare, hesitated. Sandy looked into her eyes and caught a glimmer of compassion.

For a brief moment, she thought maybe Sammi—someone–could understand she hadn't chosen to have such a ridiculous rainbow mane.

"Come ON, Sammi!" yelled Cynthia. As if under a spell, Sammi turned to join them.

Everyone listened to Cynthia.

The other seahorsicorns continued to back away slowly. Sandy's heart was pounding. She could feel tears welling behind her eyes and her chest heaved. Before she could cry, a hungry chomperfish darted in, its large, toothy mouth breaking up the gathering. He sped past her, sending her spinning head over tail into the seaweed.

Chomperfish weren't smart like seahorsicorns. Similar to the other fish of the sea, they didn't know how to talk or build neighborhoods and streets. But unlike the other creatures, they liked to gobble up the citizens of Spectra. Seahorsicorns were far too bony—not to mention hairy—to make a decent meal for most creatures. But chomperfish sunk their teeth into whatever they saw, because they could.

Sandy turned herself upright and watched the others in horror from behind blades of seaweed. A mother seahorsicorn swam furiously toward her foal, who was still in the open water. He hadn't learned how to disappear yet, and the chomperfish was coming straight for him. She grabbed his arm, pulling him away just as its jaws slammed down. They fled back to the coral in a flurry of bubbles, then vanished.

The confused chomperfish stopped, not knowing what to do next. His crude eyes skimmed the coral as he swished his tail, jerking his head left and right. For a moment he swam in place, silently floating in the water. Then, as if forgetting why he was there, he flicked his tail and left.

Once he was out of sight, the seahorsicorns reappeared one by one from the coral. "Sandy, this is your fault," Cynthia called out, not knowing where Sandy had gone. "We were all safe until that chomperfish saw you! We almost lost a foal this time!"

Sandy slid deeper into the seaweed. No one was safe when she was around, so she couldn't go by the others and eat the good plankton. Since she couldn't be with them, she feared she would always struggle to find food.

The rest of the day and into the night she was too sad to move from the seaweed. She sank down, dragged by the weight of her satchel and heavy heart until her tail hit the sandy reef floor. She didn't know how she would make it on her own.

Chapter 2:
New Hope

Sandy woke up to flickering sunlight from the warm surface as she rocked back and forth between blades of seaweed. She stretched her hooves and smiled at the new day.

While the night's rest hadn't eased her worries, it energized her to try again.

She looked around. *"Of course! This seaweed is the answer!"* She nipped away at the blade next to her, then awkwardly rolled it around her mane.

"There. Now my rainbow hair is covered up! They can't blame me for attracting chomperfish now. Why didn't I think of this earlier?"

She made her way toward open waters where currents of plankton called to her for breakfast. A couple of young mares saw her. She gave them a shy grin and waved nervously. Their puzzled faces made Sandy wonder how silly she looked. No one wore seaweed in their mane. But she reasoned that silly or not, the others couldn't complain.

"I've solved the problem of my flashy mane, which should make them feel safe. Maybe I can even make friends with them!" She took a gulp and headed their way.

At that moment, a leaf from the seaweed

wrap drooped over her eyes. With her vision blocked, her horn became tangled as she swam under an arch of coral. Pushing the seaweed away, she saw what was to blame—a cluster of dangling starflowers. *"Ugh, why are these starflowers taunting me?"*

Starflowers were beautiful, but they meant nothing to seahorsicorns. They came in every color of the rainbow, with sparkling stamen and vine-like roots that wrapped around the coral in mesmerizing swirls. There were so many covering Spectra that no one really noticed them. Curiously, the seahorsicoral—and the sea moss that dangled over the reef edge—were the only places starflowers grew. All the seahorsicorns knew was that starflowers took a long time to grow, bloomed far longer than any other flower, and once one was planted many could grow from the same root.

To Sandy, starflowers meant less than nothing. They were just another reminder of her broken magic, like the mares snickering as she untangled her horn. She brushed herself off, tried to ignore them, and continued on her way.

That's when Cynthia spotted her. "Oh wow, THIS is rich! Nice seaweed, weirdo! We still know what color your hair is under there!" She and her friends giggled and swam away. Sandy was hurt, but not surprised.

"Sandy, come here, would you?" she heard from behind a coral.

"Who on earth would want to talk to me?" she thought as she swam toward the voice. It was the mayor of Spectra hiding behind a branchy coral.

"Sandy, how are you?" she asked. Sandy raised an eyebrow in response. She wasn't asked that question often. "I have something important to talk to you about in private.'

"Now, I know your folks. They're good seahorsicorns—real fine citizens. So, it pains me to tell you this, but I think your presence here just isn't working. I have to ask you to leave Spectra."

"But... look at my hair. It's covered up. That should keep chomperfish from noticing me." said Sandy.

The mayor lowered her head before

explaining further. "I'm sorry Sandy, it's too late. After the chomperfish attack yesterday, the Spectra board members met and discussed the matter. They feel you're too dangerous. Spectra is a safe, cheerful place and we want to keep it that way. I suggest that you make your way out."

Cynthia burst through the coral behind the mayor, her friends following her. "Are you telling her to leave? GREAT idea!"

"Cynthia, this is none of your business. Have you been listening to us?" asked the mayor.

Cynthia didn't answer the mayor. With every swish of her fin, her spiteful eyes got closer. Sandy cowered in fear and slowly backed away, trying to escape. "Hey Sandy, no one wants you around. Spectra doesn't want seahorsicorns who look different!"

Sandy looked over her shoulder. They were no longer behind a coral. They were out in the open, dangerously close to the most powerful current at the edge of the reef.

"Cynthia, please stop!" cried Sammi as the others laughed.

Ignoring Sammi, Cynthia drew closer. "Why don't you leave NOW!" she said as she lunged forward.

Sandy jumped back. In an instant the current sucked her in, leaving a stunned gathering of seahorsicorns and an unraveled seaweed wrap floating behind.

She spiraled beneath the outer bank of the seahorsicoral, desperately thrashing her

hooves to grasp onto something, anything

before she completely blew away from the rocky

cliff edges below the reef.

After what felt like forever, she latched a

hoof into a rocky outcropping, but couldn't hold

on for long. The pounding current picked her up

and dragged her, then thew her with a thud.

It took a moment before Sandy noticed the water wasn't beating against her anymore. She unclenched her eyes.

"Where am I?" she thought. It took another moment to grasp whether she was right side up or upside down. She scanned the cool rock walls surrounding her. That's when she realized the current had thrown her into the safety of a short rock tunnel.

The rubble and bubbles of the current streamed past the tunnel entrance before her. As she gazed at the rushing water in disbelief, her eyes settled onto two odd shell hooks near the opening.

After a bit, she snapped out of her stare and turned to inspect the rest of the tunnel. A large, pink clamshell door was on the other end.

She swam toward it and knocked.

No answer.

She pulled the knob and looked inside.
To her surprise, she found a charming cave.
A **mother-of-pearl** clamshell bed, rock
countertops, a mirror, an ornate brush carved
from bleached coral and several decorations
lined the walls. Much of it was coated with a
layer of thick algae. Filtered light from small
seaweed-covered openings high above the cave

door softly lit the space.

"Hello?" she called. She didn't want to barge in on anyone. When no one responded, she cautiously peeked around each corner, checking for the cave's owner. No one was there.

Befuddled, she sat on a shell chair next to a polished rock table. She realized her hoof was sore and her arms were still trembling from the dangerous ride in the current. As she rested and rubbed the soreness from her hoof, a diamond-pattern net under the table caught her eye.

It looked ancient. Sandy loved historical objects, so she pulled the net out and inspected every bit of it. The weave was tight and sturdy, and the top had loops about as far apart as...
"The seashell hooks in the tunnel!"

Sandy swam to the hooks and carefully

looped the net onto them. The end of the net floated into the current and sent it billowing open. When she brought the net inside, it had already caught four plankton.

"Amazing!" she thought. *"Whoever was in this cave before me used this net to catch their food!"*

Sandy went back inside and sat down to eat and gather her thoughts. *"A cave with everything I need... no more struggling for food... no more worrying about chomperfish or what seahorsicorns think of my mane... this must be what it feels like to be blessed!"*

Chapter 3:
Questions & Answers

Sandy tossed and turned in her new clamshell bed as she tried to get sleep.

She felt sick to her stomach when she thought of her parents. Had Cynthia not chased her off, she could have said goodbye to them one last time. She had planned to visit them every once in a while, but now she couldn't see them at all.

"I wish I could tell them I'm safe in here. But then I'd have to leave, and that's not safe! I'm not strong enough to swim through the

current outside of the tunnel. And if I get swept away again, who knows where I'll end up!"

She tossed again, thinking about what she would do tomorrow inside the cave by herself. Luckily her satchel was packed with drawing supplies, books and other small hobbies.

While those projects would surely help pass the time, she was afraid she might go crazy with no one to keep her company. In the nest, her little brothers Slate and Sawyer entertained her with their wrestling matches. Her little

sister Celene said funny words like "dilly" instead of "filly." And sweet baby Silvia could always put a smile on her face with her clumsy new swimming skills. *"Now I can't see them at all..."*

"Well," she thought, *"at least I won't have to deal with Cynthia or all those other seahorsicorns who are afraid of me."*

She turned.

"Who lived here before?"

"What will I do when my octopus ink and seaweed paper runs out?"

"When Mom and Dad find out I was asked to leave Spectra, will they be disappointed in me?"

Through her storm of thoughts, she decided the safety of her new home was most important. *"I'll just have to wait to find the answers to my questions."* With that, she finally fell asleep.

* * * * * * *

Days passed. Cleaning algae from the walls with sponges she had found in the cave was a welcome cure for boredom.

She marveled at the ornate wall carvings the cleaning revealed—image after image of starflowers. Despite how she felt about them, she appreciated the carver's artistry.

While cleaning, she stumbled on the answer to one of her questions—a stash of carving tools under the counter.

"If I run out of paper and ink, I can learn to carve and add pictures to the wall!" she thought. There was plenty of space to add her own designs and keep herself busy for a long time.

While she planned beautifully carved patterns in her head, she swirled the sponge against the wall and whistled a cheerful tune.

Seahorsicorns had perfectly shaped snouts for whistling and could perform any tune with ease. They whistled together at gatherings or when they felt happy. Sandy rarely whistled because she didn't want to draw any more attention to herself. Her rainbow mane already did plenty of that. But now, in the solitude of her cave, she let loose.

She was really enjoying herself—scrubbing and whistling, whistling and scrubbing—when suddenly a knock came at the door. Her heart stopped. Prickling fear ran through her body. *"How could someone be here? Getting through that current is dangerous!"*

She heard a stallion's voice call, "Who's in there? I heard you whistling—I'm a seahorsicorn too! Would you open the door so I can meet you?"

Sandy couldn't believe her ears. No one from Spectra would be foolish enough to swim in the chomperfish-filled open waters outside the reef.

She didn't recognize his voice, and she knew better than to talk to strangers, so she kept perfectly quiet as she waited for him to leave. Eventually she felt brave enough to uncover the peephole in the door. She saw no one outside.

"Did I just imagine that?"

Later that day when she took a break to eat supper, another knock came at the door. She swam to the peephole. Again, no one was there.

"Now they're just messing with me... or

I've lost my mind." She opened the door to look around.

There at the foot of the door was a scroll with a beautiful pink starflower wrapped around it. Sandy cringed at the sight of the flower, but brought the note inside to read anyway.

Chapter 4:
Letters

"Dear Secret Seahorsicorn,

I'm sorry if I scared you earlier. I heard you whistling, and I forgot my manners because I was so excited to find a fellow seahorsicorn.

I come from a cave far away called Vigil. Nothing ever happens there, so I left to explore the sea and do exciting new things!

I've been swimming around for a while, bumping into many types of fish and covering dangerous terrain. I've been alone this whole time. You seem adventurous. How else could you explain a seahorsicorn who lives in the middle of nowhere behind a wild current? So I wanted to get to know you. Want to come out and be friends?

    - Scorny

    PS—I hope you like the flower—it's the most beautiful kind I've ever seen."

"Oh my," Sandy thought. *That was a lot* to absorb in one letter. First of all, she'd never even heard of Vigil. School taught her that the citizens of Spectra were the only seahorsicorns on earth.

"But I've never heard of a seahorsicorn named Scorny in Spectra, so maybe it's true? Still, that doesn't explain how this oddly named fellow could swim through that powerful current."

Strange as it all was, Sandy was excited at the opportunity. No one had ever wanted to be her friend before. She twirled the pink starflower in her hoof, appreciating its beauty now that it was a gesture of friendship.

"But I'm not the seahorsicorn he thinks I am, and he's still a stranger. Plus, he would surely laugh at my rainbow mane once he saw me!"

So she wrote him back:

"Scorny,

I'm sorry to disappoint you, but I'm not adventurous at all. A mean seahorsicorn chased me out of my seahorsicoral because I'm different. No one else wanted me there either. I got lost in the current and ended up here by accident. So I'm not brave! And I'm too afraid to leave with that nasty current out there. So I'm just going to stay put. I'm sorry if that's not very interesting.

If you're looking for an adventurous seahorsicorn, you might find one in Spectra. Have you been there yet? It's just above the rocky cliffs. Maybe you saw it when you picked the lovely starflower. Spectra is covered in them. Thank you for that, by the way.

I really could use a friend, though. How would you feel about being pen pals?

- Sandy

PS—How did you get past the current?"

Sandy rolled up her letter and placed it just outside the door. Then she went about her business, eagerly waiting for another knock at the door.

It was early afternoon the next day when she heard the knock. She checked the peephole and, again, saw no one. She opened the door and found another note, this time wrapped with a beautiful yellow starflower.

"Dear Sandy,

The seahorsicorns in Spectra sound mean and lame. You seem interesting though, even if you aren't adventurous. Maybe we can work on that! So yes, I'd like to be your pen pal. Thank you for asking!

- Scorny

PS—When you're an adventurer, wild currents are fun!"

Part 2
TRUTHS

Chapter 5:
Scorny

Scorny pricked his ears at the sound of distant clacking. In the open sea, attacks came on suddenly, so it was important to stay alert for potential threats. As long as the clacking came from far away, he knew he wasn't disturbing any of the ill-tempered lobsters who made their homes between the boulders far below Spectra. New base-dwelling creatures were a regular hazard on his way to the compartment he'd created to stash his letters from Sandy.

It wasn't in his nature to save things. Adventurers pack light and aren't tied down by unnecessary objects. But Sandy's letters were special to him.

It felt like ages since she had intrigued him with her first letter. The seahorsicorns he had known from Vigil wouldn't have admitted they were an outcast, or weak. Her honesty was refreshing.

Scorny strained as he pushed and pulled at boulders to create an opening large enough to slide her letter through. He hadn't thought about how he would get the letters out, but he wasn't much of a planner. That, among other flaws, had been drilled into his head since he was a colt.

Scorny hadn't been able to sit still, listen,

or focus in school. Or home. Or at all. Vigil was a giant cave, surrounded not just by chomperfish, but by many frightening deep-sea fish. There were strict rules about how noisy or excited its citizens could get. As long as nearby predators couldn't hear a peep, everyone was safe. It was their way of protecting themselves. But those were Vigil's rules, not Scorny's.

The others were frustrated with his outbursts and lack of cooperation. The more his teachers, classmates, parents, or the entire seahorsicoral told him to settle down, the more he felt like he would explode.

"*Someday,*" he said to himself, *"I'll get out of this lifeless cave and swim the open sea!"*

When he became a young stallion, he crept out of Vigil and never looked back. His quick wit, fast reflexes and desire for excitement—all the things that made him a horrible citizen of Vigil—made him an excellent explorer.

He had been through plenty of scrapes and had the scars to prove it. But as long as he was swimming in the open sea, he didn't mind. He didn't know where he was going or what he was looking for, but now he wondered if it had been Sandy.

Always up for a new challenge, he made his next adventure meeting Sandy. His mission was to see her face to face, and that meant learning friendship skills adventurers rarely need: patience, gentleness and thoughtfulness.

He reasoned that if he stayed nearby and did thoughtful things, he would prove himself to be trustworthy. *"Perhaps then she'll leave her cave and join me."*

He grinned to himself as he glanced at her letter one more time. She was busy with a new carving project—a seashell pattern she had designed herself and sketched at the bottom of the page in painstaking detail. After he slid the letter through the crevice he had created, he set out to write his reply. This meant swimming to Spectra to pluck the daily starflower.

At first, he had gathered starflowers from the long, mossy arms that draped over Spectra's reef cliff. When those were gone, he moved into

the seahorsicoral, eventually plucking his way to the center of the reef.

Based on what Sandy explained in her first letter, Scorny wasn't interested in meeting the seahorsicorns of Spectra. So he kept to himself and snuck from coral to coral to avoid being noticed. But he often caught a glimpse of them.

They were not like the seahorsicorns from his home. The first time he saw them he marveled at how they floated carelessly in the open with their coats of peach, lemon yellow, minty green, periwinkle, lavender and pink, and manes to match their bodies. He sometimes wondered how Sandy looked. She said she was different from everyone else, but everyone in Spectra seemed different to him.

The citizens of Vigil were covered in deep, rich **indigo** as dark as night, with bright, neon colors at the tips of their hooves and manes. They looked almost exactly like the luminescent coral that lit up their cave. Scorny's mane sported a shocking electric green.

"Darn, what color did I get for her yesterday?" he thought as he scrounged for a starflower in a patch of seaweed. He never used to think about frivolous things like colors. But Sandy was artistic, and he figured that might be important to her. He finally settled on a periwinkle starflower. As he reached to pluck it from the cluster, a commotion broke out several coral away.

"GET IT AWAY FROM ME!"

Scorny looked through the seaweed in time to see a yellow seahorsicorn thrashing through the water above the coral. A toothy, open-mouthed chomperfish was close on her tail. Not far behind, a pink seahorsicorn chased the chomperfish, waving a shiny, silver shell.

"OVER HERE!" the pink seahorsicorn shouted. As the distracted fish spun around, she tossed the shell over her head, then dove into the coral before the chomperfish spotted her. As it crushed the hard shell into a cloud of debris with its jaws, the yellow seahorsicorn swam to safety.

"Clever," Scorny thought to himself as he watched the chomperfish swim away, unaware that he hadn't caught an actual meal.

Scorny had often wondered how the open-water seahorsicorns of Spectra protected themselves. Until that moment, he never witnessed a chomperfish attack. The pink seahorsicorn was almost compelling enough for Scorny to introduce himself, but he thought better of it. *"Sandy said these guys kicked her out. Even if they seem brave, they're not nice."* He plucked the starflower and made his way to the reef edge. *"Well, now I know what I'll write about in my letter."*

Scorny wasn't one to conjure up deep, artistic thoughts for his letters like Sandy. Some days he had trouble coming up with new things to write. Usually all he could think to tell her about was his adventures in the reef. Nothing unusual had happened to him that day, so the chomperfish attack in Spectra was his only inspiration.

He settled down to compose his letter inside a rocky nook he had found along the cliff edge. It was a useful space that provided some shelter not far below Sandy's cave. With his pen hovering over the page, he stared at the rough walls and wondered how to start. Just as in school, his eyes glossed over and his mind wandered.

Then, in the corner of his eye, he spotted a skinny orange tentacle curiously groping the floor near his tail. Scorny quietly pulled a rope from his bag, gathered several twisted shells from the ledge next to him and waited.

Chapter 6:
Creature Comforts

Sandy unraveled a blotchy periwinkle starflower from Scorny's note. The note itself was unusually dirty and heavy. As the letter rolled open, several twisty, grimy turritella shells slid out and floated onto the table with a tink, tink, tink. She giggled out loud. Today's letter would be good. She could tell Scorny had battled an ink octopus and gathered some of its spoils. He always put their ink into the same tiny brown shells so she could stash them away and refill her writing pens. *"He must have really scared this one,"* she thought. *"Three whole shells!"*

Sandy had grown to appreciate Scorny's letters. Not just because she was alone in the cave, but because of his kind gestures.

She also admired his battle stories. It seemed as if he had grappled with every type of creature below the reef—chomperfish, crabs, jellyfish, barracuda, and a gnarly looking giant starfish, to name a few.

Her eyes lit up as she read every detail of his fight against the octopus on the cloudy, ink-stained page, sometimes laughing out loud at his unusual methods.

"... once the octopus realized I tied his tentacle up in my rope, he got real angry. That's when I remembered the other seven tentacles. They were whipping around like mad! The ink was already all over the place and I was running out of time if I wanted to get any of it into my shells.

I had found a dead sea urchin the other day while I was swimming through the cliffs and thought it might be useful. I wasn't sure how I would use it at the time, but I figured it out pretty quick today.

With one hoof, I was trying to hold the octopus down. With the other, I was feeling around the walls for where I had hung the urchin.

It poked my arm. First I thought, 'Ouch!!' but then I thought, 'Good, I found it!' I put it on my head just before the octopus took a swing at me. He let out a big yelp when he hit my new helmet, and then the other tentacles took a turn. He just kept swinging and yelping and squirting ink everywhere!..."

Sandy had a good belly laugh, then added the blotchy starflower to one of the many conch shell vases Scorny had given her. Bouquets covered the table and lined the walls, wrapping Sandy in the feeling of friendship she'd never had in Spectra.

Letter after letter arrived at her door, each with a new story of open-sea adventure—1,284 to be exact. She kept an organized stack of them in a drawer with her stationery.

As she added the letter and ink shells to the pile, she worried he would get fed up with her cowardice. *"He seems fearless, and I'm too scared to leave the cave!"*

"But why would I?" she reasoned, *"it's much easier to stay safe and well-fed here than it ever was in Spectra."*

"*Because you miss your parents.*"

"*Because you haven't watched your little siblings grow up. Slate has to be 12 by now. That would make Sawyer 11. Celene would be 8, and sweet little Silvia must be 5. You're missing it all.*"

"*But they're probably safer without me.*"

Sandy argued with herself every day, and safety won out every time. Or fear. She wasn't sure. Besides, the only time she ever had a friend was while she lived in the cave, and she didn't want to lose that. That's why she never told him about her rainbow hair, her broken invisibility magic or starflower-creating powers.

And she never asked him to bring a letter to her family.

"*If I ask him to deliver a letter to my*

family, he might ask the citizens of Spectra for directions. Everyone hates me there. They could turn him against me... or worse, he could run into Cynthia!"

She brushed off her hooves and got back to work on the clamshell carving she had started on the other side of the cubbyhole—the only part of the walls that had room left for ornamentation. She had covered all the other spaces.

She finished her chisel work and polished her pattern with the scratchy sand Scorny

found many letters ago when she first wrote to him about her carving hobby. After buffing the ridges of the clamshells for a while, her hoof became tired, so she took a moment to lean back and observe her work.

"That's enough for today. Tomorrow it will be finished."

Chapter 7:
Spectra

Sandy had been polishing well into the afternoon when she heard a loud knock.

"Sandy? It's Scorny. I know we never talk through the door, but this is important."

Sandy's heart stopped. "What is it?" she said as she swam toward the door to hear him more clearly. She was surprised at her voice. She hadn't heard it in some time.

"The seahorsicorns in Spectra found me today while I was picking you a flower," he said gruffly.

Sandy's heart went from stop to go, pounding hard in her chest. *"They must have convinced him I was dangerous—just like I was afraid of!"*

"Who found you?" she asked.

"All of them, probably. It seemed like every seahorsicorn in Spectra was there."

"Oh…" said Sandy. "What did they say to you?"

"Most of it is in this letter," he said as he slid a flat, unrolled note under the door. "They asked me to bring it to you."

Sandy's shaking hoof scooped up the note. Her mind raced as she turned it over. She saw what looked like all the seahorsicorns' signatures on the bottom of the message. One stood out more than the rest—Cynthia.

"This can't be good," she thought as she swallowed the lump in her throat.

"Sandy?" Scorny asked, snapping Sandy out of her thoughts.

"What is it?"

"Why didn't you tell me you could make starflowers?"

"I... I didn't think it mattered," she said.

"This whole time I was bringing them to you, you could have made your own."

She had never thought about it that way. "I suppose you're right," she admitted.

"What a sucker I've been!"

"What? Why?" Sandy said. Now her heart was somewhere on the floor. "How?"

"I was trying to be a friend and bring thoughtful gifts so you could trust me and I

could meet you some day. You could have made your own starflowers. Did you ever plan to come out of there? I'm an adventurer, Sandy. I could have kept moving and having more adventures, but I stayed here because of you."

"Wait—" Sandy said, dismayed, "I love your letters, the beautiful starflowers and all the thoughtful gifts you bring, because they're from you! I wasn't trying to trick you. I'm just scared to leave the cave! I'm sorry I didn't tell you about my magic. It wasn't about the starflowers or the gifts. It was about your friendship!"

"You also didn't tell me the seahorsicorns in Spectra use magic to disappear," said Scorny.

Sandy was confused. "Everyone knows about disappearing magic. I'm the only seahorsicorn who can't disappear. That's part of why I've stayed in the cave, Scorny. If I try getting past that current, I'll be swept to who-knows-where with dangerous creatures and I won't be able to disappear!"

A moment passed. "Scorny?" Sandy asked.

"Not everyone knows about disappearing magic, Sandy. I didn't know about disappearing magic. Not until today. I've been out here this entire time with no magic!"

Sandy's mind reeled. She had assumed he was protected by the same magic as the rest of the seahorsicorns. "How could you not know about disappearing magic?" she asked.

"Read the letter, Sandy."

"Ok," she said meekly.

"The others hope you'll come back to Spectra."

"They do? That can't be possible–" Sandy began.

"I'll come back tomorrow and help you get through the current if you can get past your fear. But if you're too afraid to come out... I don't know if I'll stick around this reef anymore."

"Scorny, please don't be angry. I just need some time to figure things out..." said Sandy.

"You've had a lot of time," said Scorny. "You need to decide. You have to STOP BEING A COWARD!"

The words cut Sandy like a knife. She didn't fully understand what was going on, but she knew what he said was true. She had been protected by the cave and pampered by Scorny's gifts long enough. Using him to stay safe while he swam in chomperfish-infested waters was not an equal friendship.

Sandy heard Scorny take a breath on the other side of the door. "Like I said. I'll be back again tomorrow." As usual, by the time she looked through the peephole, he was already gone.

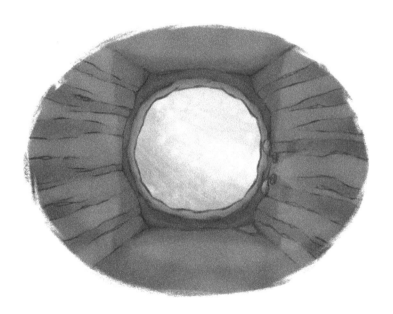

Chapter 8:
The Truth

"Dear Sandy,

We're sorry we were cruel to you. We shouldn't have voted for you to leave Spectra. That was wrong. We should have tried to help you instead.

Since you've been gone, your friend Scorny has been picking the starflowers and there aren't many left.

We had so many before that we never knew how important they were. This whole time we thought we had the power to disappear, but as the starflowers vanished, we started losing our magic. We didn't know what was happening at first, but then we figured it out: if we're near a starflower we can disappear; if we're far away, we can't.

Chomperfish can see us now, and we can't hide, just like you.

There isn't enough time to grow more starflowers, and you're the only one who can make them appear instantly with magic. Will you please come back and use your important gift to help us?

We thought you were gone forever until we met Scorny. We didn't appreciate you, and we regret it. We are deeply sorry. Please come back and give us another chance."

Sandy leaned against her mother-of-pearl headboard and took it all in.

"They want me. My magic is useful!" she thought to herself in disbelief.

She really was blessed by the Great Spirit. She had respect and finally knew her purpose. But it was all overshadowed by Scorny's anger toward her. Her head was spinning. Good news, bad news, starflower magic, Scorny.

Now it made sense why Scorny was so upset. Since he came from Vigil, and Vigil had no starflowers, he wouldn't be aware of disappearing magic.

"STOP BEING A COWARD!
STOP BEING A COWARD!
STOP BEING A COWARD!"

The words echoed over and over in her head. He expected her to be brave enough to join him. She had no excuse for being cowardly if he could survive on his own without magic.

Her heart ached as she realized that by hiding to protect their friendship, she may have destroyed it.

Sandy wallowed in shame over her spineless behavior as she laid in her bed. Rolling back and forth, she slowly convinced herself to be brave and leave the cave. *"You can get through that current, Sandy! Scorny will be here to help!"*

Then she shot straight up in her bed. *"What if the letter is a trick?"* She jumped down and began pacing the floor. *"What if Cynthia convinced the entire town to write it and it's all just a lie? They were so mean in the past, and this news is just too good to be true. What if they just want me to come back so they can laugh at me again?!"*

She wished there was some way to know for sure if the letter was telling the truth.

"Ugh! I have to at least try to help Spectra. It's the right thing to do, whether it's a trick or not! That settles it," she thought as she stopped mid-pace. *"I'm leaving to help Spectra AND to be a better friend to Scorny."* As she looked up from where she stood, the mother-of-pearl bed shimmered and reflected her multi-colored mane back to her. *"Oh no," she thought. "I forgot about my stupid rainbow mane! What will Scorny think? He doesn't know how ridiculous I look! No matter what I do, I could lose everything!"*

Sandy felt something she had never

felt before. Frustrated that there was no clear answer, her ears turned hot. She scanned the room, then angrily lunged toward her carving tools and grabbed the chisel.

"YOU THOUGHT THIS WOULD BE

FINISHED TODAY!" she shouted at herself as she stabbed her clamshell carving.

"YOU RUINED EVERYTHING WITH YOUR ONLY FRIEND!"

Stab.

"YOU'RE TOO AFRAID TO DO ANYTHING!"

Stab.

"NO MATTER HOW IMPORTANT YOUR MAGIC IS YOU'LL ALWAYS HAVE THIS RIDICULOUS MANE!"

Crash!

Sandy pulled her head back from the wall in shock. The fierce stabbing had sent her entire arm through the carving.

"But that's impossible," she thought to herself. *"Unless this wall is... hollow?"*

Sandy pulled her arm out and peered into the cavity it created.

"A secret compartment!"

Inside, the fading sunlight caught the corner of an ancient-looking book. She jabbed her chisel around the hole to create a larger opening, then snatched it.

On the cover and along the spine was an engraved word: "STELLA."

Sandy opened it to the first page.

Chapter 9:
Stella

"Dear Journal,

    This is a record of my separation from Spirit. I miss him, and I try to take care of his creation every day. The small village in the reef above me voted, and they agreed it would be best if I remained hidden for a while to protect my gift."

    Sandy rubbed her forehead. *"This seahorsicorn—Stella—does she mean the Great Spirit?"* she wondered. She kept reading:

"All of us are given special gifts. That's why we need each other.

I make starflowers for the seahorsicorns to keep them safe, but I can't disappear like the rest of them. That's why the new village of Spectra had their most skilled builders and craftsmen create this beautiful cave that protects me and provides all the food I need.

The adventurous seahorsicorns in the bunch volunteered to brave the dangerous waters and collect my starflowers. I look forward to seeing them and hearing how things are going, but I can't wait to see everyone else when I finally join them again someday in Spectra.

They tell me the starflowers cover the center of the village. I won't stop creating them until the entire coral is covered. I don't know if

Spirit will make another seahorsicorn like me, so I need to make more than enough flowers to provide disappearing magic for future fillies and colts."

Sandy finished the last line of the page. She never thought there could be another seahorsicorn with starflower magic like hers. She scrambled toward the letter Scorny had delivered from Spectra. Her eyes rapidly scanned the page. It all made sense. It had to be true.

Then she noticed a small message muddled between the signatures she had missed before.

"We love you and we're proud of you, Sandy. We're so glad you're OK. Please come home.—Mom & Dad"

Sandy sat and cried confused, happy tears as the cave became dark all around her. She knew what she had to do.

Chapter 10:
Leap of Faith

Sandy had just finished tidying up her cave when she heard the knock.

"Scorny!" she called. She dove for the door, threw it open and leapt out. Before her stood a stunned seahorsicorn who looked different than she had imagined.

"You... you look different than what I thought!" she said, scanning his indigo coat and electric hair. "I've never seen a seahorsicorn who looks like you!"

After a moment, Scorny's mouth curved into a grin. "Sandy! I'm so glad you came out!" He gave her a hearty hug.

"So you don't think I'm too different?" Sandy asked timidly.

He pulled away and laughed. "Are you kidding? Of course you are! I thought the other seahorsicorns were colorful, but no one is as colorful as you!"

"And that's… OK?" Sandy was not expecting to hear that.

"Sandy, adventurers don't swim around looking for the same thing every day. You're more than OK. Who would have figured I'd find the rarest seahorsicorn in all the sea?!"

"Oh," she said, blushing. She wasn't used to hearing positive things about her appearance.

"Well, um, I wanted to tell you something," she said, looking at the ground. "I'm sorry I've been such a coward for so long. You've been very patient with me and I–"

"Hold on, Sandy," Scorny interrupted. "I have something I need to tell you. Of all the seahorsicorns I've ever met, you've been the most thoughtful, and the only one willing to be my friend. Yesterday I was upset, but it didn't feel right. So I tried to be like you and really think about the situation. I realized it was wrong to be angry. I shouldn't have expected you to join me out here just because I gave you gifts. That's not how friendship works. So... will you forgive me?"

"Only if you forgive me for hiding safely in the cave while you were out in the open with no disappearing magic!" said Sandy.

"Of course," he said.

"That settles it then. Now, about that current," she said, starting down the tunnel.

"Wait, did you want anything from the cave? Now is the time to get it," Scorny said.

"No," said Sandy. "I'm going to leave that cave and everything in it behind, including my fears! I'm not scared anymore!"

Scorny raised an eyebrow and looked at her in disbelief.

"Ok, I'm scared out of my mind. But I'll stop acting scared." Sandy admitted.

"You figured it out!" said Scorny. "Being brave isn't about having no fear, it's about facing your fear."

Sandy smiled at Scorny. Then her face lit up. "I guess there is one thing I should bring!" She dashed into the cave and came back with the ancient book. "Do you think there's room for it in your travel bag? I think it's an important part of seahorsicorn history."

"Sure," Scorny said as she handed it to him.

"Stella," he read off the cover. "Looks like a classic." He stuffed it into his pack, then led Sandy by the hoof to the tunnel entrance.

"I've been afraid of this for a long time," she said.

"Well, I'm right here in case something goes wrong, and I'll help you swim through it. But first, a tip. Currents go somewhere. You have to roll with where they're going."

"How do you do that?" asked Sandy.

"Dive in with purpose. Jump into the current's path and don't fight it. Just ride with it until you've swum completely across."

"Won't that mean we'll be swept to somewhere we don't want to go?" asked Sandy.

"Only if you don't want to go there," said Scorny with a wink.

Sandy gave Scorny a wary look, then said, "Alright, pen pal. Let's do this."

Scorny swung Sandy's hoof back and forth. "1... 2... 3!"

The two dove into the current together. It pounded on Sandy and pushed her body downward, but this time she felt more control as she swam with it and pushed her way to the other side. Their outstretched hooves broke through first, then the rest of their bodies. The pounding water let up, and they were floating carefree on the other side.

"WOOOHOOOO!!" she shouted, pumping a hoof above her head. "Uh, I mean, that went a lot better than last time," she said, looking down in embarrassment from her outburst.

"That's the spirit," Scorny said with a

grin. "Now, how about we head to Spectra?"

As the two swam up the rocky cliffs, they passed the tunnel entrance. Sandy stopped. "Wait a second. How do you get into the tunnel?"

"That takes a little more timing and skill," Scorny chuckled.

Sandy looked around her. The sea was scary, but also breathtaking. She could finally see how far the sparkling surface stretched

before it disappeared from sight. Below them the rocky sea floor connected cliffs together to form an underwater valley. Silhouettes of large fish, dolphins, and jellyfish floated silently from reef to unexplored reef.

"Amazing, isn't it?" said Scorny as if reading her mind.

"Yes. I wish I hadn't been afraid of it for so long."

As they started off again, another thought entered Sandy's mind. "Scorny, how did everyone in Spectra treat you? They mistreated me because I look different, but you look different, too. Weren't they mean to you?"

"They weren't," he said. "Maybe they learned their lesson from the way they treated you."

Sandy spotted the draping sea moss arms that cascaded over the reef edge and knew they were close. The moss looked different without starflowers. Above them, she saw Sammi peering over the edge. Her face lit up at the sight of Sandy and Scorny. She turned and yelled, "They're here! They're here!"

Chapter 11:
Homecoming

Sandy felt unprepared to see everyone again. She braced herself as she and Scorny floated over the cliff edge and into the coral.

All the citizens of Spectra were there. First Sandy saw the mayor, then many familiar faces, including the stallions and mares she remembered from her school days. Sandy was a little embarrassed at all the attention, but that faded when the crowd parted and she saw the two faces she missed most of all.

"MOM! DAD!" she yelled with her arms open. She nearly knocked them down with the force of her hug. Joyful cheers erupted all around them.

"We missed you so much," said her dad.

"We're glad you've been safe this whole time. We didn't know what to think when you went missing!" said her mom.

"I'm sorry I didn't come back sooner. I'm sorry I didn't write to you," said Sandy. "I was a coward, and that hurt you!"

"It's alright, Sandy. The important thing is that you're here now," said her mom.

"Sandy!" said a little voice. She released her parents and looked down. Her little brothers and sisters stood waiting for hugs. Silvia had her arms up in the air, ready to be scooped up.

"Silvia, you're so big!" Sandy said as she lifted her. They all shared a group hug. "You're all so grown up!"

"Scorny's cute. Are you going to marry him?" Silvia said loudly. Her brothers and sisters giggled as Scorny's ears perked up.

Sandy could feel her cheeks getting warm as she laughed. "Silvia! That's not appropriate."

A tap on her shoulder interrupted them. Sandy set Silvia down and turned to find Cynthia.

Her eyes had softened. There were no traces of anger or glimmers of spite. "I'm sorry I was so awful to you," Cynthia said. "When we lost our ability to disappear, I got chased down by some chomperfish, and it made me realize how cruel it was to laugh. I should have helped protect you from them instead."

"You were pretty terrible," Sandy said, "and helping would have been way better than laughing. But if you hadn't chased me off, I would have never found out that my magic serves a purpose.

'I know what it's like to feel upset at myself. You don't have to feel that way anymore. I've started over and that includes my relationship with you."

"Thank you Sandy," Cynthia said.

They looked around. The entire crowd was silent, watching the two of them for their next move.

"Well, let's get out of the open and show you something we should have made for you a long time ago!" Cynthia said on behalf of the

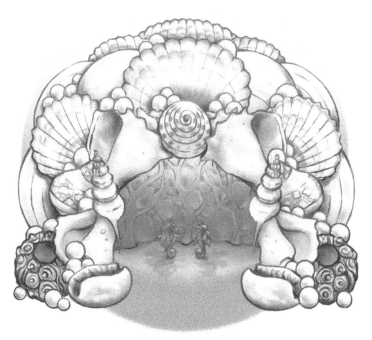

crowd. Cheers erupted again as she led Sandy
to a structure the citizens of Spectra had made.
Sandy swam inside and observed the sturdy
shell walls.

"We wanted you to have a safe place
to hide from chomperfish while you create
starflowers. You'll still make them for us, won't

you?" asked Cynthia.

"Of course I will!" Sandy said with an eager smile.

She closed her eyes, her horn shimmered, and the water around her sparkled. Starflowers appeared throughout the structure and began to float down.

Overjoyed, the seahorsicorns whistled happy tunes and swam in and out, collecting the floating starflowers and dutifully placing them throughout Spectra's coral.

Sandy opened her eyes and looked around. She saw Sammi reaching and waiting for a starflower to float down. As it touched her hooves, she swept it up and tied it into her mane.

"Sammi, that looks so pretty in your hair!" said Sandy.

Sammi looked at her with a crafty grin, then vanished. Sandy bolted upward. "Sammi, you're brilliant!"

Cynthia, who had also seen what happened, shouted to the others, "Everyone, if you put the starflowers in your hair you can disappear from anywhere!"

The idea caught on instantly. With Sandy and Sammi's help, every citizen of Spectra could disappear from wherever they were, not just near the coral.

She turned to Scorny, who had made his way to her side after taking in the spectacle.

"Spectra is better off now than before!" he exclaimed. "Look at all the amazing things you're doing for your seahorsicoral. I'm proud of you for coming out of the cave," he said, patting her on the shoulder.

For a moment Sandy became worried. "Scorny, you plan to stay, don't you? I'll be living in Spectra now. That won't be too boring, will it?"

"Ha! Far from it. You still can't disappear, and you'll need someone... ehem... adventurous to show you how to kick chomperfish tail and tackle the open sea.

'Besides, your friendship is the best adventure I've ever had. And I don't see it ending anytime soon."

Algae: simple underwater plants with no roots

Colt: a young male horse

Conch shell: a light brown shell that, when empty, has an opening that allows you to "hear the sea"

Coral: an underwater animal that looks like a plant and provides shelter for many small sea creatures

Crevice: a small opening or crack

Current: a steady flow of water

Debris: small pieces

Filly: a young female horse

Foal: a young horse, male or female

Indigo: blue and purple mixed together

Intrigued: having caused interest or a feeling of curiousness

Lavender: light purple, or purple and white mixed together

Luminescent: a cold glow

Mare: an adult female horse

Mother-of-pearl: a colorful layer on the inside of some shells that is made of the same material as pearls

Ornamentation: decoration

Periwinkle: blue, purple and white mixed together

Plankton: small animals that float through water and are eaten by many sea creatures, including whales and seahorses

Satchel: a bag similar to a purse, but worn with a strap across the body instead of over the shoulder

Scroll: rolled paper with a written message

Seahorsicorn: a magical underwater creature that is a unicorn on the top and a seahorse on the bottom

Seahorsicoral: a coral reef where seahorsicorns live

Sea Urchin: a spiny creature that can be found in coral reefs

Sibling: brother or sister

Stallion: an adult male horse

Stamen: the whisker-like part of flowers that grow from the center

Turritella shell: a tightly coiled, skinny cone-shaped shell

Depending on when you catch her, Jessica Kopecky is a graphic designer, architectural photographer, mural artist, illustrator, craft pattern creator, wife and mom. While designing a stuffed toy inspired by her daughter, things got a little out of control until—whoops—she had developed an entire enchanted undersea world... and became an author-illustrator in the process.

The adventure doesn't stop here!

Go to www.secretofthestarflower.com to join the community!